Unstuck Together

written by

Aarti Love Mahtani

Illustrated by

Marco Zerneri

How to read this book

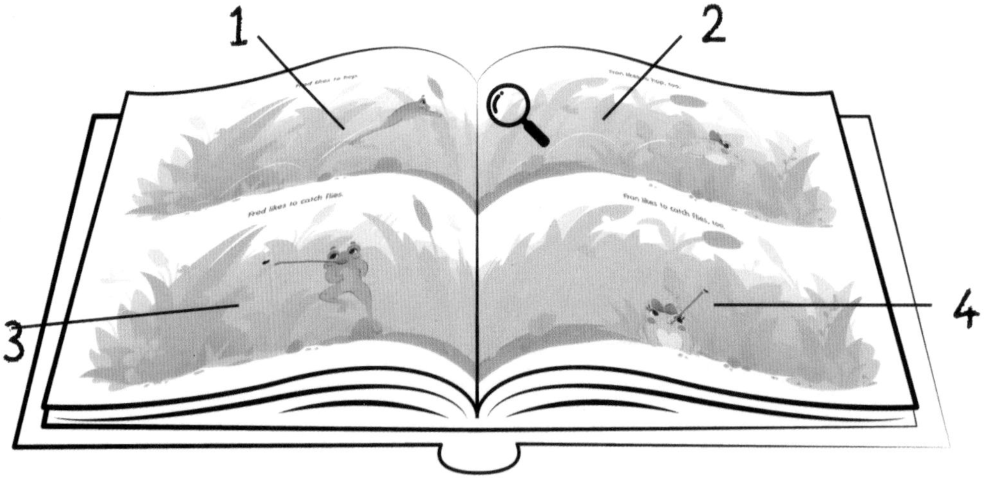

Fred and Fran are best friends.

They live in a little pond.

They do everything together.

Fred likes to hop.

Fred likes to catch flies.

Fran likes to hop, too.

Fran likes to catch flies, too.

Fred and Fran hop together.

They hop as high as they can.

They hop sideways.

They even hop and flip upside down!

As they hop, they spot a fly.

They both hop towards the fly, ready to catch it.

Crash!

Smash!

Fred and Fran collide into each other
and the fly escapes!

Fred pulls away.

Uh oh!

Fred tugs.

Fran pulls away, too.

They are stuck!

Their tongues are tied!

Fran tugs harder!

The more they tug, the tighter the knot becomes.

Fred croaks.

Fred is tired.

Fran croaks louder!

The more they croak,
the less they can hear each other.

Fran is tired, too.

Fred is on one side of the little pond.

Fred feels sad.

Fran is on the other side of the little pond.

The pond is small, but they feel very far apart.

Fran feels sad, too.

Fred hops closer.

Fred croaks and cries.

Fran hops closer, too.

Fran croaks and cries, too.

The closer they get, the looser the knot becomes!

Their tongues are untied!

Fred is happy!

Fran is happier!

Fred smiles.

Fran smiles back.

Fred hops high!

Fran hops higher!

Fred and Fran are best friends. They do everything together.

They hop together.

They catch flies together.

They get stuck together.

And they even get
unstuck together.

For Om & Vishal
I love you both infinitely.
-A.L.M.

For Otter,
With whom I got unstuck together.
-M.Z.

unstuck together

Story by Aarti Love Mahtani - Illustrations by Marco Zerneri
Layout and graphic design by TACOM - Creative Studio

ISBN: 979-8-35091-371-2

Find Fred and Fran's friends hidden in the story:

- [ ] Ant
- [ ] Butterfly
- [ ] Caterpillar
- [ ] Dragonfly
- [ ] Earthworm
- [ ] Fish